3

Cat flew over the town.

Cat on the
Magic Mat

by Karen Wallace and Mette Engell

Cat flew over the house.

Cat flew over the farm.

Cat flew over the hill.

9

Cat flew over the river.

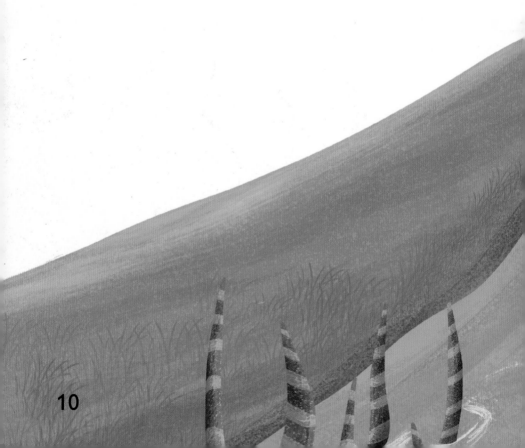

Cat flew over the sea.

13

Cat flew over the castle.

Cat flew over the bridge.

Cat flew over the house.

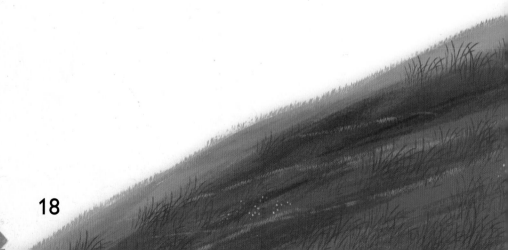

19

Story trail

Start at the beginning of the story trail. Ask your child to retell the story in their own words, pointing to each picture in turn to recall the sequence of events.

Start

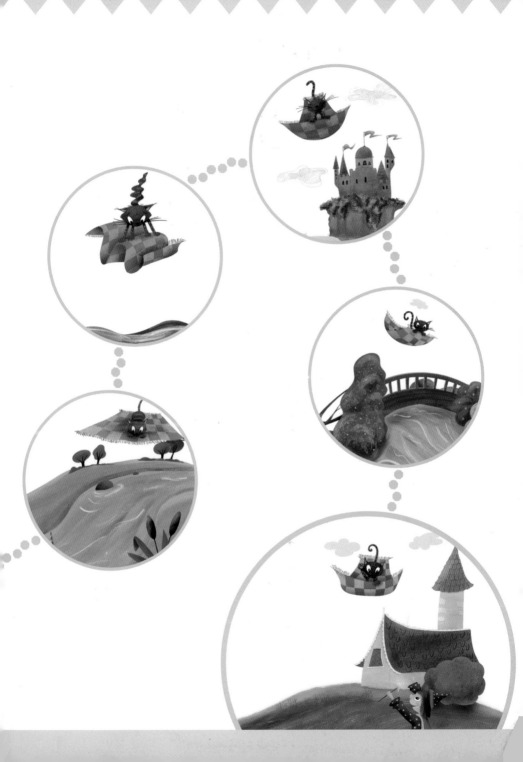

Independent Reading

This series is designed to provide an opportunity for your child to read on their own. These notes are written for you to help your child choose a book and to read it independently.

In school, your child's teacher will often be using reading books which have been banded to support the process of learning to read. Use the book band colour your child is reading in school to help you make a good choice. *Cat on the Magic Mat* is a good choice for children reading at Pink 1B in their classroom to read independently.

The aim of independent reading is to read this book with ease, so that your child enjoys the story and relates it to their own experiences.

About the book
In this story, a cat gets a ride on a magic mat, and is very pleased to land back at home again.

Before reading
Help your child to learn how to make good choices by asking: "Why did you choose this book? Why do you think you will enjoy it?" Support your child to think about what they already know about the story context. Look at the cover together and ask: "What do you think the story will be about?" Read the title aloud and ask: "What do you think the mat will do?"

Remind your child that they can try to sound out the letters to make a word if they get stuck.

Decide together whether your child will read the story independently or read it aloud to you. When books are short, as at Pink 1B, your child may wish to do both!

During reading

If reading aloud, support your child if they hesitate or ask for help by telling the word. Remind your child of what they know and what they can do independently.

If reading to themselves, remind your child that they can come and ask for your help if stuck.

After reading:

Support comprehension by asking your child to tell you about the story. Help your child think about the messages in the book that go beyond the story. Ask: "Do you think Cat expected the mat to fly up into the air? Do you think Cat enjoyed the magic mat ride?"

Give your child a chance to respond to the story: "Did you have a favourite part? If you could make something magic, what would it be?" Use the story trail to encourage your child to retell the story in the right sequence, in their own words.

Extending learning

Help your child extend the story structure by using the same sentence pattern and adding some more elements: "Cat might have flown somewhere else before coming home. Cat flew over the school. Cat flew over the park. Now you think of one."

On a few of the pages, check your child can finger point accurately by asking them to show you how they kept their place in the print by tracking from word to word.

Help your child to use letter information by asking them to find the interest word on each page by using the first letter. For example: "Which word is 'house'? How do you know it is that word?"

Franklin Watts
First published in Great Britain in 2019 by The Watts Publishing Group

Series Editors: Jackie Hamley and Melanie Palmer
Series Advisors: Dr Sue Bodman and Glen Franklin
Series Designers: Cathryn Gilbert and Peter Scoulding

A CIP catalogue record for this book is
available from the British Library.

ISBN 978 1 4451 6750 3 (hbk)
ISBN 978 1 4451 6752 7 (pbk)
ISBN 978 1 4451 6751 0 (library ebook)

Printed in China

Franklin Watts
An imprint of
Hachette Children's Group
Part of The Watts Publishing Group
Carmelite House
50 Victoria Embankment
London EC4Y 0DZ

An Hachette UK Company
www.hachette.co.uk

www.franklinwatts.co.uk

For Nico and Lizie
– K.W.